DATE DUE

FEB 0 2

APES

ANIMAL FAMILIES

APES

Annemarie Schmidt and Christian R. Schmidt

Gareth Stevens Publishing
MILWAUKEE

A N I M A L   F A M I L I E S

For a free color catalog describing Gareth Stevens' list of high-quality books, call 1-800-341-3569 (USA) or 1-800-461-9120 (Canada).

The editor would like to extend special thanks to Jan W. Rafert, Curator of Primates and Small Mammals, Milwaukee County Zoo, Milwaukee, Wisconsin, for his kind and professional help with the information in this book.

Picture Credits

M. Badham—13 (beeloh), 20; Bruce Coleman—13 (gray gibbon, silvery gibbon, white-handed gibbon), 18, 23, 25 (right), 27, 37 (lower); Hans D. Dossenbach—cover, 13 (orangutan); Jacana—4 (right), 5, 7 (right), 13 (chimpanzee, agile gibbon), 15, 17, 19, 26 (lower), 36; Krenger—10; A. Meder—31 (upper); Midgard—2; NASA—11; Natural History Museum, London—9; M. Neugebauer—40; NHPA—13 (hoolock), 21, 37 (upper); Photo Researchers—13 (bonobo), 38, 39; Ringier—6; Christian R. Schmidt—1, 4 (left), 12 (upper and lower), 13 (siamang, white-cheeked gibbon, capped gibbon), 14, 16, 22 (left and right), 24, 25 (left), 26 (upper left and right), 28, 30, 31 (lower), 32, 33, 34 (all three photos), 35; Silvestris—13 (gorilla), 29.

Library of Congress Cataloging-in-Publication Data
Schmidt, Annemarie.
 [Menschenaffen. English]
 Apes / Annemarie Schmidt and Christian R. Schmidt.
  p. cm. — (Animal families)
 Translation of: Menschenaffen.
 Includes bibliographical references and index.
 Summary: Examines the characteristics and natural environment of various members of the ape family, including gibbons, gorillas, and chimpanzees.
 ISBN 0-8368-0840-1
 1. Apes—Juvenile literature. [1. Apes.] I. Schmidt, Christian R. II. Title. III. Series.
QL737.P96S3713 1992
599.88—dc20   92-10659

North American edition first published in 1992 by
Gareth Stevens Publishing
1555 North RiverCenter Drive, Suite 201
Milwaukee, Wisconsin 53212, USA

Series editor: Patricia Lantier-Sampon
Editor: Charles R. Bennett
Translated from the German by Jamie Daniel
Editorial assistants: Diane Laska and Aldemar Hagen
Editorial consultant: Jan W. Rafert

Printed in the United States of America

1 2 3 4 5 6 7 8 9 98 97 96 95 94 93 92

Table of Contents

What Is an Ape?

For many centuries, apes were thought to be bad-tempered, dangerous monsters. Even in this century, the film King Kong portrays the gorilla as a violent, wild beast.

Apes are often the favorites of visitors to a zoo. Maybe you've seen the powerful male gorilla with its silver back, the orangutan with its long, red hair, the young chimpanzees with big ears, or the gibbons that play for hours without tiring. People everywhere are fascinated by these animals and have spent long moments watching them, enjoying their tricks and playfulness. It is amazing to note how much the behavior of apes seems like ours. We have seen their faces show human feelings — anger, pleasure, surprise, curiosity, and fear. Probably because apes are so much like humans, we sometimes feel as if we understand them.

Similar — But Not the Same

Of all the animals, apes are most like humans. Apes have longer arms and shorter legs than people have, but when apes stand up straight, no one can deny their human similarities. The long arms and short legs of the apes are specially suited to their particular way of life and their environment.

Apes all resemble humans in some way. But apes and people don't just look alike; their muscles and organs are similar, too. Scientists have also found that the blood of humans and apes is similar. In addition, humans and apes share ways in which they differ from other animals. For example, neither humans nor apes have tails, nor do they have a protective undercoat beneath their hair. Also, apes and humans do not instinctively know how to swim when they are born. And, although siamangs can swim

and are fairly good at the breaststroke, few other apes learn to swim. This may be one reason why gibbons and large apes in zoos are sometimes kept on islands in ponds. There, they can be easily seen by visitors but can't run away.

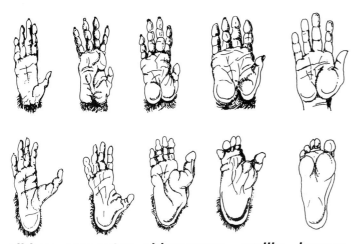

gibbon orangutan chimpanzee gorilla human

In many ways, the larger, or great, apes resemble humans more than they do the smaller, or lesser, apes. For example, it is easy to see that a baby ape's behavior, games, and stunts are very similar to those of a human child's. Soon, however, the baby ape climbs up curtains, throws flowerpots, and does other things it might do if it were in its natural forest home. These activities are a reminder that apes are not human. And in spite of all the similarities, apes live different kinds of lives than humans do. This book will show just how apes' lives are different and how they exist both in the wild and in captivity.

M'Pungu and Ensego

In ancient times, not much was known about animals that lived in faraway lands. In most cases, the only information available had been reported by sailors or traders. Many of these reports were not accurate, and the sailors often added details from their imagination. The first accounts of apes go back about twenty-five hundred years. At that time, a sailor named Hanno sailed from Carthage in northern Africa along the west coast of Africa. When he returned, he told stories of "wild people in animal skins." Hanno had probably come in contact with gorillas.

Toward the end of the sixteenth century, an English pirate named Andrew Battel sailed along the coast of the Congo. He reported seeing "two types of monster." One was called "M'Pungu" or "Pongo." It was "a giant covered with hair, with the face of a man and the comprehension of an animal." The second type was called "Ensego." Battel said it was smaller but was "extremely dangerous." Battel had probably seen gorillas and chimpanzees.

place animals of the world into various groups. He put humans, apes, and monkeys into the same group, called *primates*. About a hundred years later, Charles Darwin wrote a book called *On the Origin of Species*. He claimed that apes and humans both came from the same ancestors. Many people did not believe his theory. Scientists then began to search for bones and other fossils. They wanted to prove or disprove Darwin's ideas. That search

gibbon   **orangutan**   **chimpanzee**   **gorilla**   **human**

The first reports of orangutans came from Malaysia in about 1750. In the language of Malaysia, *orangutan* means "person of the forest." The people living there thought these red apes were able to speak but chose not to in order to avoid work.

The Search for Old Bones
Carolus Linnaeus was the first scientist to

is still going on, but scientists today have more information and better views of how humans might have developed. Some experts think that one ancestor of apes and humans was *Proconsul africanus*. This extinct ape lived in the forests of eastern Africa about twenty million years ago. Fossils tell us how these creatures looked and moved but not how they lived. Over time, some of these apes

Right: **The** Proconsul africanus *that lived in East Africa between 17 and 22 million years ago was the common ancestor of both apes and humans.*

began to change in appearance. The gibbons, or lesser apes, were the first to develop their own characteristics. Next came orangutans, then gorillas, and finally chimpanzees. All this happened between eight and twenty million years ago. But humans developed only about half a million years ago, so they are still rather young on the evolutionary scale. Because of this fact, some scientists thought it might be a good idea to learn about humans from the study of modern apes.

The Wrong Picture

For a long time, apes were the subject of human fear and mockery. In the early part of the twentieth century, people understood very little about apes. In fact, many people thought of apes as half-human monsters. For example, in a U.S. movie, King Kong was a fearsome, giant gorilla that was half human and half beast. Yet, people were fascinated by the apes, so many of these animals were captured and put into circuses or carnivals for public viewing. They were dressed in human clothes and made to do tricks, such as walking a tightrope or sitting at a table and eating like people.

Even zoos did not at first understand the apes' most basic needs. The animals were often kept alone in small cages and were fed human food. Apes in the wild naturally eat fruit and plants. But in the zoos, they were fed bread and butter, gravy, sausage, or ground meat. As a result, apes often became overweight and were unhealthy. Many died after only one or two years of zoo life.

The Zoo as a New Home

Happily, modern zoos do a much better job of caring for apes. Today, people try to make zoos as much like animals' real homes as possible. Apes have a lot of space and get the same kind of food they would eat if they were in their native forests.

Apes in today's zoos do not have to worry about enemies or finding food. As a result, they do not get as much exercise as they would in the wild. So zoos try to provide apes with activities and materials to keep them busy. Visitors might see apes swinging on tires hanging from ropes or playing with boxes, burlap bags, or even newspapers. Apes might use some of these materials to build sleeping nests, just as they would if they lived in the wild.

At one time, apes in captivity were kept alone. But this meant that no young would be

born. Today, zoos try to keep apes in groups that are the same size as they would be in their natural home. Now, babies are being born, and zoos do not have to capture apes from the wild. Now, many orangutans and chimpanzees are born in zoos around the world. Also, the number of gorillas born in zoos is increasing. And beautiful gibbon babies, peering out from their mothers' hair, are always among the most popular animals at the zoo.

Foster Apes
Experts believe that young female apes learn

to be good mothers by watching older, more experienced females care for their children. But sometimes young apes are separated from their mothers. This can happen if the mother doesn't have enough milk. Also, the mother sometimes makes her baby leave. This usually happens when the mother is very young.

When this happens, the baby becomes a kind of foster child. It may even begin its life in a human family. This works quite well, since in many ways the baby ape needs the same things a human baby does. It must have milk every few hours. Later, it is given cooked cereal and fruit to eat. Also, a lot of time is spent playing with the baby ape. If the baby ape is treated this way, it will soon be able to return to its own family.

Used — and Abused

Not all apes in captivity have this simple life. Sometimes apes are used as "substitute people." Because chimpanzees are so much like people, they are often used in experiments to test new medicines. One famous chimpanzee was named Ham. In 1961, he flew into space in a rocket. After the flight, Ham lived in the zoo in Washington, D.C. Chimpanzees are sometimes used in movies or television programs to entertain audiences. But this kind of treatment can be bad for young chimps. If they are kept away from a zoo too long, they won't be able to take care of themselves when they are returned.

Gibbons can have similar problems. These animals are often bought as pets. People who buy them mean well, but gibbons do not like being pets. Sadly, after a while as a pet, a gibbon usually has a hard time living in a zoo.

Talking?

It is clear that apes can communicate with

each other. Various sounds and gestures they make mean very specific things. Some apes have even been taught words. One gorilla, Koko, learned and uses over three hundred signs from the sign language used by deaf people. Apes, however, could never

11

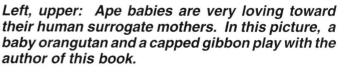

Left, upper: Ape babies are very loving toward their human surrogate mothers. In this picture, a baby orangutan and a capped gibbon play with the author of this book.
Left, lower: A baby gorilla contentedly drinks from a bottle.

learn human language. For one thing, their brains are not developed enough. Also, apes' vocal chords are not made to pronounce human words.

This does not mean that apes are not smart. Apes have been given intelligence tests and have come up with excellent solutions to complicated problems. For example, when apes have several sticks, they know to use the longest one to reach food that is far away. Some apes have even connected two sticks to reach food they couldn't reach with one.

The Future of Apes

Scientists now know more about apes than ever before. So it seems especially sad when we look at the apes' future. All the great apes and four kinds of gibbons are endangered species. This means these animals could completely die out. The main reason the apes are threatened is that their forest homes are being cut down by humans. People are using more and more lumber to build things and more and more grazing land for their cattle. This means they have to cut down trees. Every year, about 1.3 million acres (540,000 ha) of forest are cut down in the world.

In order to combat this problem, zoos all over the world now keep breeding records and have breeding programs. This way, the numbers of apes in zoos will increase. But the programs won't mean very much if we don't also save the natural homes of the apes. Without enough forests, apes will be lost, and zoos will become simply museums.

White-handed Gibbon

Agile Gibbon

Gray Gibbon

Silvery Gibbon

Capped Gibbon

Kloss' Gibbon

A Guide to Apes

White-cheeked Gibbon

Hoolock

Siamang

Orangutan

Gorilla

Chimpanzee

Bonobo

13

Lesser Apes

The lesser apes, or gibbons, make their home in the dense rain forests of Southeast Asia. There, like trapeze artists, they swing with lightning speed from branch to branch through the treetops, sometimes up to 30 miles (50 km) per hour. The scientific word for their hand-over-hand swinging is *brachiation*. Their long fingers and long, powerful arms are well suited to this swinging. Gibbons spend about 90 percent of the time they are awake swinging in the trees. To get from one tree to another, gibbons can "fly" up to 40 feet (12 m). In the air, they seem almost weightless. They do have accidents, though. About one out of three gibbons has had a broken arm or leg, probably from falling.

Gibbons are arboreal, which means they almost never leave the trees, even to get a drink. When they are thirsty, they hang from a branch that stretches over a stream and scoop up handfuls of water. They also suck the water from their wet hair.

When gibbons walk on the ground, they may stand up straight and walk on two feet. In this position, their long arms come down to their ankles. Gibbons and humans are the only two animals that can walk upright this way for long distances. Sometimes, the gibbons walk holding their arms up and out to the side to keep their balance, or they may use their arms as crutches when they need to move quickly.

Gibbons sleep in the forks of tree branches. They eat fruit, leaves, buds, blossoms, insects, and birds' eggs. They pick up food with their hands and then put it into their mouths.

Male and female gibbons are about the same size, and a pair will stay together for life. About every two years, the female has a baby. The gestation period — the time it takes the baby to grow inside the mother — is about seven months. At birth, the baby has very little hair. For about four months, it clings to its mother's hair. Everywhere the mother goes, the baby also goes. After four months, the baby can hang from a branch. At six months, it tries its first steps. A young gibbon stays with the family for five to eight years. Once it becomes an adult, a female child is driven away by the mother and a male by the father. When a gibbon finds its own territory, it announces that fact with loud calls. The calls also help the gibbon find a mate.

Gibbons' natural enemies include leopards, yellow-throated martens, snakes, and large birds of prey. Their worst enemies are humans. People are constantly cutting down the forest environments that the gibbons need to survive.

White-handed Gibbons

Scientific name: Hylobates lar
Weight: 11-18 pounds (5-8 kg)
Height seated: 17-25 inches (44-64 cm)

With its arms balanced carefully at its sides, this young white-handed gibbon can walk upright on the ground.

The white-handed gibbon is also called the lar. It is found mainly in southern China, eastern Burma, Thailand, and on the Malay Peninsula. It has also been seen on the northern tip of the island of Borneo. The thick hair of the white-handed gibbon protects it from the cold and damp in the high mountain forests it lives in. The hair color of males and females varies from beige to brown to dark brown to black. Their hands and feet, however, are always white. Light and dark white-handed gibbons often mate. The offspring they produce are always either completely light or dark. That is, they are never a mixed, or in-between, color.

White-handed gibbons swing high in the trees. They may be seen as high as 100 feet (30 m) above the ground. They were first studied in 1937 by Clarence Ray Carpenter, who spent time researching their everyday life. The day begins at about six or seven o'clock. The family group starts the morning by singing. The male and female take turns, and together they make one distinctive melody. Next, they set out together to look for food. They eat about 250 different kinds of plants. Each day, a gibbon eats about one-sixth of its body weight in food. At midday, the group takes a break. During this time, they rest and play before starting out again. The day ends late in the afternoon. By that time, the gibbons will have covered about one mile (1.6 km) in their search for food.

There are more white-handed gibbons in zoos than any other type of gibbon. They are very attractive animals, and at one time, tourists to Southeast Asia actually bought them to keep as pets. But the animals are not suitable to keep; they do not like life as pets and do not thrive in such an atmosphere. Most of the baby gibbons bought as pets died soon after they arrived at their new home.

Taking a baby gibbon out of its natural environment would not only disturb the health and welfare of the baby. It would also completely upset the life of the gibbon mother, since mother and child are especially close to one another during the first year of the baby's life. In this sense, an entire family would be affected by a forced separation. It is now illegal for anyone to have a white-handed gibbon as a pet.

Agile Gibbons and Gray Gibbons

Scientific name: Hylobates agilis *(agile gibbon);* Hylobates muelleri *(gray gibbon)*
Weight: 11-13 pounds (5-6 kg)
Height seated: 17-25 inches (44-64 cm)

surrounds the entire face. The only sure way to tell the two apart is by their songs. The agile gibbon begins its song in a deep voice. As the song continues, the pitch rises higher and higher. The gray gibbon's song is always at a very high pitch.

The homes of the two gibbons are suited to each other's needs. The gray gibbon lives on

This agile gibbon can be recognized by its distinctive singing pattern.

The agile gibbon and the gray gibbon look almost alike. Even zoologists have trouble telling them apart. Because of their similarity, many believe that the gray gibbon is a subspecies of the agile gibbon.

The agile and the gray gibbon (also called Mueller's gibbon) may be light or dark. Usually, the agile gibbon has darker hands and feet. Both species have a band of bright hair above the eyes. Sometimes the band

the island of Borneo except for the southwestern tip, where the agile gibbon lives. The agile gibbon also lives on the Malay Peninsula and on all but the northern tip of Sumatra, where the white-handed gibbon lives. The gray gibbon needs about one and one-half times as much territory as the agile gibbon. Yet the gray gibbon travels much less than the agile gibbon. Scientists have not been able to explain why this happens.

Silvery Gibbons

Scientific name: Hylobates moloch
Weight: 11-13 pounds (5-6 kg)
Height seated: 17-25 inches (44-64 cm)

been a worldwide effort to save the animal.

Silvery gibbons live in thirty-five of the sixty-three forested areas on Java. It is estimated that there are about 2,400 to 7,000 animals living there. They start their day before six o'clock in the morning. A few hours later, the females begin to sing a warning to other gibbons to stay away from the territory.

Male silvery gibbons rarely make calls; only females make great-calls — loud calls that make their location known to other gibbons.

The silvery gibbon is the most endangered of all the gibbons. It lives only in the rain forests of western Java. At one time, there were about 12,640 square miles (32,740 sq km) of forest in this area. Today, there are only about 290 square miles (750 sq km) of forest. This means that the silvery gibbon has lost more than 97 percent of its territory. Using breeding records and programs, there has

If other gibbons do enter, however, the silvery gibbons defend their area by scratching and biting the invaders. Silvery gibbons are active for about eleven hours of each day.

Baby silvery gibbons are born with cream-colored coats that change to gray as they mature. Adults usually have at least a small area of black coloring, called *capping*, on their heads and sometimes on their throats.

Capped Gibbons

Scientific name: Hylobates pileatus
Weight: 10.5-15 pounds (4.5-7 kg)
Height seated: 17-25 inches (44-64 cm)

The capped gibbon lives in eastern Thailand, Cambodia, and southern Laos. Like the silvery gibbon, the capped gibbon is an endangered species. For many years, people have fought wars in the area, and food shortages have forced the people who live there to hunt the capped gibbon for food. In addition, huge sections of the forest have been destroyed by the wars. Today, the forests in eastern Thailand are reduced by 20 percent each year.

The young capped gibbons have soft, light-colored hair. Females stay light in color their entire lives, but as adults they develop a black breast and a black cap. When males become adults, their coat turns black. The big difference in the color of the male and the female often causes people to think these gibbons belong to different species.

Because the capped gibbons have white hands and feet, it was once thought they were a subspecies of the white-handed gibbon. Blood tests, however, proved the two were different species. The white-handed and capped gibbons live next to one another. And about one out of ten family groups has a mixed pair. The male capped gibbon sometimes mates with a female white-handed gibbon. The opposite, however, does not occur. In fact, sometimes a male capped gibbon has one mate of each species.

Although adult capped gibbon males have black coats, females are beige in color.

Capped gibbons eat plants, although many prefer the fruit to the leaves. This makes it easy for zoos to keep plants for the gibbons, since the plants do not die. One of the capped gibbons' favorite foods is figs. It is amusing to see them carrying the figs in their feet, as they use their hands to hang from the branches.

Kloss' Gibbons

Scientific name: Hylobates klossi
Weight: 11-13 pounds (5-6 kg)
Height seated: 17-25 inches (44-64 cm)

Even later, when Kloss' gibbons were hunted, their numbers were not in danger. But the human population of the islands eventually became five times larger. At the same time, guns and hunting dogs were introduced in the islands. From that time on, the Kloss' gibbon has been threatened with extinction.

The only Kloss' gibbon living outside its natural habitat seems happy at Twycross Zoo in England.

The Kloss' gibbon, a black gibbon, is also called a beeloh. It was once called the dwarf siamang, because it looks so much like the larger siamang, another black gibbon that lives in Sumatra and on the Malay Peninsula.

The Kloss' gibbon lives on the Mentawai Islands, southwest of Sumatra. People there once believed that the souls of their dead lived on in the bodies of the Kloss' gibbons. For this reason, the animal was never killed.

A Kloss' gibbon family usually lives in a territory of about 27 acres (11 ha). About three-fourths of its food is the fruit of plants. Since fruit is much harder to find than leaves, it is surprising that the Kloss' gibbon lives in such a small area. The rest of its diet consists of insects, which makes it difficult to feed these animals in a zoo. A Kloss' gibbon family often covers a little over one mile (2 km) a day looking for food.

Hoolocks

Scientific name: Hylobates hoolock
Weight: 12-15.5 pounds (5.5-7 kg)
Height seated: 17-25 inches (44-64 cm)

a throat sac. When it fills with air, the animals' voices are very loud. Singing usually takes place in the hours just before noon, with both males and females capable of making a great-call. Unlike white-handed gibbons that usually call while swinging, hoolocks call while sitting on a branch.

A hoolock male sings while sitting on a leafy branch in its treetop home.

The hoolock lives in Assam, Myanmar (Burma), and eastern Bangladesh. Males are black and have white stripes above their eyes. Females are light brown, with a complete face-ring. Hoolocks can be found in mountain forests at altitudes as high as 1,400 feet (427 m). Their long hair protects them during the cool mountain nights.

Hoolock pairs mark their territory by singing. Both male and female hoolocks have

Most of the hoolock's food is fruit. These animals also eat leaves, blossoms, and shoots. Occasionally they eat insects. There are very few hoolocks in zoos outside their native lands. It sometimes happens that zoos think they have hoolocks when they actually do not. That is because of the similarities among the small gibbons species. The coloring is especially confusing, since it depends not only on sex but on age as well.

White-cheeked Gibbons

Scientific name: Hylobates concolor
Weight: 12.5-15.5 pounds (5.5-7 kg)
Height seated: 17-25 inches (44-64 cm)

risks from the sprays, so they do not know much about the white-cheeked gibbon.

White-cheeked gibbons are light beige when they are born. By the time they are a year old, they turn black. When the females are five or six years old, they again turn beige. Scientists have divided white-cheeked gibbons

A black white-cheeked gibbon male (left) and a light-colored female with her baby (right).

The white-cheeked gibbon is also called the crested gibbon. It lives in Laos, Vietnam, eastern Cambodia, southern China, and on the island of Hainan. This gibbon is an endangered species. Hunting has reduced its numbers. And much of the forest where it lives has been destroyed, mainly by the poison sprays used in the long wars fought in these areas. For years, scientists could not go into this geographical region because of the health

into six subspecies. Three live in the northern areas, and three live in the south.

A zoo in Mulhouse, France, is trying very hard to save the species. This zoo has records of all white-cheeked gibbons living in zoos all over the world. Some day it may be possible to send some of these gibbons back into the wild. Before that can happen, however, a special section of forest must be available for this purpose.

Siamangs

Scientific name: Symphalangus syndactylus
Weight: 20-34 pounds (9-15.5 kg)
Height seated: 29.5-35 inches (75-90 cm)

It is easy to tell the siamang from other gibbons because it is larger and stronger. The siamang lives on the Malay Peninsula and the island of Sumatra. It shares its home with the agile and white-handed gibbons.

The second and third toes of the siamang sometimes grow together. This occasionally happens to other gibbons as well. Scientists do not know why this happens. Siamangs swing through the trees at heights of about 80 to 100 feet (25-30 m). They aren't as fast as the smaller gibbons, but they are still very agile and elegant.

The siamang eats different foods than other gibbons. It prefers the leaves, sprouts, and blossoms of plants. This means that it is much easier for the siamang to find food since it can harvest foliage from the giant trees that make up its home territory. Other gibbons prefer fruit and have to look harder and longer for their food. Since the siamang's food is so easy to find, it is happy with smaller territories than other gibbons. A siamang may have to travel only half a mile (.8 km) to find its food for the day. Siamangs also eat a small number of insects.

Siamangs are the champion singers of the gibbon world. They have large sacs on their throats. When they fill the sacs with air, their voices become extremely loud. Their voices can be heard up to about 2 miles (3 km) away. Every three days, siamangs sing their song in the morning, usually between 8:00 a.m. and 10:00 a.m. Each pair of siamangs has its own song with a specific pattern or melody, and these songs warn other siamangs to stay away. The singing continues as the siamangs swing from branch to branch.

Young siamangs also sing. Their singing attracts mates. This way, when it is time for the young siamang to leave the family, it has already found a partner in the neighborhood.

All siamangs spend a large part of their

Siamangs inflate their throat sacs while singing.

time grooming one another. Most of this grooming activity takes place during resting time and also when the animals settle in at the end of the day.

The female siamang has a new baby about every two years. As each new baby is born, the male siamang then takes care of the older offspring. In a group, siamangs travel in single file, and members of each family follow similar routines during the day.

Great Apes

Orangutans

Scientific name: Pongo pygmaeus
Weight: Male, 200-265 pounds (90-120 kg)
   Female, 90-110 pounds (40-50 kg)
Height seated: 30.5-38 inches (78-97 cm)

Orangutans are the largest mammals that live in trees. They live on Borneo and northwestern Sumatra. There are two subspecies of orangutan. Those that live on Sumatra have long, narrow faces. The males have pear-shaped jowls that are covered with light-colored hair. They have orange hair that can grow as long as 50 inches (130 cm). The orangutans that live on Borneo have dark brown hair, and their jowls are shorter. Males are about twice as large as females. Females are full grown at ten years of age.

The Borneo males are the largest orangutans. They weigh up to 265 pounds (120 kg) in the wild and even more in zoos. Their size often works against them when they climb. For

Opposite : A young orangutan on Borneo, not yet fully grown.
Above: Differences between the two orangutan subspecies are apparent in these two large males: Sumatran males (left) have a "well kept" beard and light-haired jowls. Males on Borneo (right) have a very large throat sac and are often fat.

25

this reason, Borneo orangutans spend more time on the ground than Sumatran orangutans. This can be dangerous. On the ground, they are prey for tigers and Malaysian wild dogs, clouded leopards, and pythons.

When orangutans move on the ground, they use a "fist" walk. They keep their hands balled up into fists at their sides. It is funny

to watch baby orangutans learning to walk, with their shoulders up and their arms held almost straight out for balance.

The big orangutans spend most of the day and all night in the trees. They never leap, but instead climb carefully, holding tightly with both hands and feet. If they want to go to another tree, they make a branch bend until it is close enough to the other tree for them to jump safely over.

Because their only home is in the forest, the destruction of forests is a serious threat to orangutans. In 1974 alone, for example, about half of the forests of Sumatra were cleared. Every year since then, about a thousand orangutans on both islands have lost their homes.

Until about 1950, many orangutans were captured for zoos. Some were also kept as pets by the islanders. As a result, special stations for training orangutans to live once

again in the wild were organized. The first was on northern Borneo in 1965, and others followed. Two Swiss women, Monica Borner and Regina Frey, started the Bohorok station. They have helped hundreds of pet orangutans return to life in the forest.

Each night, an orangutan makes a sleeping nest in a tree, most often from branches and

Above, left: "Please don't leave me alone!" But there's no reason to worry. This little orangutan can now calm down again (right).

Like gorillas, chimpanzees, and bonobos, young orangutans nurse for about three years.

leaves. Sometimes they build platforms with a roof made from a giant leaf to protect them from the rain. Scientists have used these nests to estimate that there are at most thirty thousand orangutans in the wild.

Orangutans sometimes use tools while looking for food. They use long sticks to knock down fruit they cannot reach. Fruit makes up about two-thirds of the orangutan diet. They also eat young leaves and shoots, bark, lianas, mineral-rich soil, insects, and sometimes even birds' eggs or young birds and squirrels.

As a rule, apes are patient and loving mothers. But like human mothers, they must also sometimes be strict with their children.

Orangutans leave their sleeping nests about an hour after sunrise. They have to travel only a few hundred yards to find their day's food. On Sumatra, one might see groups of about fifteen orangutans in a single tree eating fruit. Sometimes they follow animals such as hornbills, pigeons, and other birds to help them find such trees.

Except for those gatherings, orangutans usually stay alone. If any are seen together, it may be a mother and her young. It could also be a male and a female who stay together for several months while they are mating. A male's territory may be up to 4 square miles (10 sq km). Within the area, there may be separate territories of up to twenty females.

To keep other males away and to attract females, a male puffs up his throat sac and makes loud, shouting noises. Occasionally, two males do meet. Usually, they do not fight. Instead, they try to frighten each other by staring, shouting, and shaking branches.

Every four to six years, the female gives birth to one baby. Its gestation period is about eight months. The baby, with its funny tufts of hair, holds tightly to the mother's hair so it won't fall as she climbs through the trees. The baby depends entirely on its mother for all of its needs for a year after its birth. The mother feeds the baby, protects it, sleeps near it, and spends time grooming the young orangutan. A female bears about five or six young in her lifetime. The young nurse for three years, but they eat food after four months. They become adults when they are about ten years old. Male orangutans have no responsibilities toward their offspring.

Orangutans no longer have to be captured for zoos. Each year, about fifty orangutans are born in captivity around the world. The ape that lived the longest in captivity was an orangutan — a Sumatran male in the Philadelphia Zoo that lived to be fifty-nine years old. In the wild, orangutans live about thirty to forty years. Orangutans are an endangered species. Their habitats are steadily being destroyed by human industry and hunting.

Sumatran orangutans prefer to stay in the trees.

Gorillas

Scientific Name: Gorilla gorilla
Weight: Male, 330-440 pounds (150-200 kg)
   Female, 155-220 pounds (70-100 kg)
Height: 4'5"-5'5" (140-170 cm)

The gorilla is the largest of all the primates. A gorilla that is 440 pounds (200 kg) of solid muscle can be a fearsome sight. But gorillas are not the violent, wild beasts many people think they are. In fact, we now know that gorillas are peaceful animals that rarely become aggressive. A male gorilla can get excited when he wants to frighten a rival and defend a female. Then he stands up straight, presses his lips together, stares, and beats his hands on his chest. However, gorillas that don't know one another usually stay out of each other's way.

Gorillas prefer to walk on all fours. And unlike the orangutans who use their fists when they walk, gorillas curl under the first two joints of their fingers. The skin there is a tough hide. This method of movement is called knuckle walking.

There are three gorilla subspecies. The western lowland gorilla lives in west-central Africa. It is thinner and has longer legs than the other species. It has short, brownish gray hair. Scientists estimate that there are sixty thousand of these gorillas alive today. Almost all the gorillas in zoos are of this type.

The eastern lowland gorilla is found in the eastern part of Zaire. It is larger than its relatives and has a longer face. There are only about four thousand of these apes living.

The black mountain gorilla lives in the heart of Africa where the borders of Zaire, Rwanda, and Uganda meet. The mountain gorilla is in the greatest danger. There are only about six hundred of them left on earth, and none of them are in zoos. Mountain gorillas have long, thick hair that protects them from the cold, damp air of the mighty mountain forests. Over the years, the animals have had to move higher and higher into the mountains. That is because people have

Adult gorillas make an imposing impression by beating their chests.

taken over more and more of the forests for farmland. In these higher regions, where it often gets near freezing, mountain gorillas sometimes die from pneumonia.

Gorillas like to live in sunny woods where there is a lot of undergrowth. They spend about 90 percent of their time on the ground. Babies and younger animals like to play in the trees, but grown males rarely climb trees. Usually, about ten gorillas live together as a family. The group may, however, have as many as thirty-five members.

Each group is led by one silverback. When a male gorilla is about twelve years old, the hair on its back begins to turn gray, or silver. There are from two to twelve females and their young in a family. There may also be several half-grown, black-backed males. Sometimes an older leader allows a younger son to act as a second silverback. Then, if something happens to the leader, the son is ready to take over the family.

A family's territory ranges from about 2-11.5 square miles (5-30 sq km). The edges of the territory overlap with the territories of neighboring families. A family covers between one- and two-thirds of a mile (0.5-1 km) to find the day's food. Sometimes when families meet, females from one family will become members of the other.

Gorillas sleep on the ground. Each evening, they make a new sleeping nest and sleep for up to thirteen hours. The babies don't build nests. They sleep with their mothers.

Male mountain gorillas often help care for their young.

Gorilla babies like to suck their fingers — it doesn't have to be a thumb!

Gorillas wake up an hour after sunrise. The silverback decides the speed and direction of the day's activities. The animals then spend most of the day eating. The adults might take a break to rest or sunbathe, while the young animals play. Mountain gorillas eat more than one hundred types of plants. Their favorites include bedstraw, wild celery, nettles, and thistles. They also like bitter leaves, bamboo shoots, wood pith, and bark. They eat about one-tenth of their body weight in food each day. A tiny bit of this food is snails, worms, or insects.

Lowland gorillas sometimes wade into rivers and eat water plants. They eat much more fruit than the mountain gorillas do. Since fruit is harder to find, the lowland

Female gorillas often grow quite stout, even in the wild. Western flatland gorillas have "caps" with a great variety of colorings.

gorillas live in smaller family groups. This way, there are fewer mouths to feed.

When female gorillas are about ten years old, they begin to bear young about once every four years. Their gestation period is eight and one-half months. They almost always have one baby, although the birth of twins has been recorded. The mothers carry the young in their arms. Baby gorillas can't hold on to the mother's hair the way gibbons and orangutans can, but when they are a little older, the young ride piggyback. Silverbacks are good fathers. They sometimes care for the one- to two-year-olds. Then the mothers have more time to eat, which means they will produce more milk for the young.

And as the baby grows up and is healthy, the mother will be favored by the silverback.

Other than humans, gorillas have no enemies. In Rwanda and Zaire, some gorilla families have grown used to human visitors. The governments charge the visitors fees, and the money goes toward protecting the animals and their homes.

The first gorilla to be born in a zoo was Colo. She was born in the Columbus, Ohio, zoo in 1956. Goma was the first European-born gorilla. She was born in the zoo in Basel, Switzerland, in 1956. Colo and Goma later became mothers themselves. The oldest gorilla in captivity was Massa in the Philadelphia Zoo. Massa lived to be fifty-four years old.

A silverback, such as this western flatland gorilla, won't just beat his chest to look impressive. Sometimes, he will also walk upright.

Chimpanzees

Scientific name: Pan troglodytes
Weight: 88-175 pounds (40-80 kg)
Height seated: 27.5-36 inches (70-92 cm)

Of all the apes, the chimpanzees are most humanlike. This likeness, however, is often a disadvantage for chimpanzees. For example, chimpanzees can catch human diseases. And for this reason, they are often used in medical research. In many zoos, chimpanzees — as well as other apes — are kept behind glass panels instead of bars. This protects them from catching an illness from one of the zoo's visitors.

There are about 150,000 chimpanzees living in the wild. This may seem like a large number. However, many chimpanzees are captured for medical research. Also, their natural homes are steadily being destroyed. If both activities continue at the same pace, the number of chimpanzees will soon be drastically reduced.

Chimpanzees are divided into three subspecies — West African, Central African, and East African. They live in fifteen different countries from Senegal to Tanzania.

Chimpanzees live in rain forests and in the bush- and tree-covered savannas. They spend about one-third of their time in trees, where they love to make long leaps and swing with

This West African male chimpanzee is taking it easy on a branch.

their arms from one branch to another. On the ground, chimpanzees walk on their knuckles like gorillas. Males are somewhat larger than females and have strong incisor teeth, which they use when they fight.

Older chimpanzees often have gray beards and bald foreheads. This almost makes them look like bald-headed humans. Young chimpanzees have light-colored facial skin, giant ears, and eyes that glisten with mischief.

Chimpanzees are highly intelligent and can communicate with each other through various gestures and movements that are similar to humans. When two chimpanzees meet after a long separation, for example, they will most often greet with pursed lips and "kiss" each other. Also, after a fight, one chimpanzee might reach out and stroke the other's hand as if to say "Let's be nice to each other again." The chimpanzee language also has a lot of different sounds. These sounds can range from soft grunts the animals make while eating to wild screeching, hooting, and shouting that can be heard over half a mile (1 km) away.

Chimpanzees spend about four hours a day eating fruit. As is true of orangutans, groups of hungry chimpanzees gather in the branches of a single tree, feasting on the fruit. Each evening, before they build their sleeping nest in a tree, chimpanzees will eat a meal of leaves and shoots. Depending on where they live, chimpanzees may have over four hundred kinds of plants from which to choose. If plants aren't available, chimpanzees will eat cotton seeds, blossoms, resin, and even bark. Termites, ants, and sometimes even meat are part of the chimpanzee diet.

Except for human beings, no other animals make and use as many tools as the

Young chimpanzees are intelligent and have curious, entertaining personalities. Their light-colored faces can be just as expressive as those of humans.

chimpanzees. They often use some sort of tool to help gather food. In the Ivory Coast, females use hammers and anvils to break open nuts. First, they gather stones into a pile. Then, they put the nuts into a hollow in the pile where they crack the shells. Chimpanzees also use branches to stir up ant hills. They then scoop up the scrambling insects with a lightning-quick movement. By using this method, they avoid painful ant bites. To get termites out of their colonies, chimpanzees first remove the leaves from a stalk or a twig. Next, they poke it into one of the entrance holes. They then enjoy plucking

This young chimpanzee feels quite secure in the company of adults.

the termites with the stick one by one. To drink water, chimpanzees often use chewed-up leaves, which they dip into the water and use like a sponge. They also use leaves as washcloths. And after a meal, the chimps often use a small twig as a toothpick. The fact that chimpanzees recognize their own reflections in a mirror is another indication of

young no longer nurse, but they stay with their mothers for several more years.

Chimpanzees live in large groups, or communities. A group has from fifteen up to as many as 120 members. A community this large needs a territory of between 3 and 5.7 square miles (8-15 sq km). Females wander about 1.5 to 2 miles (2-3 km) every day, but

how highly their intelligence is developed.

Male chimpanzees don't usually use tools to look for insects. Instead, they hunt young baboons, monkeys, boar, and antelope. When a male catches his prey, he shares the meal with his friends.

Chimpanzees are full-grown when they are between eight and twelve years old. Females give birth to one offspring about every five years. The gestation period is eight months. Twins are rare, and there has been only one known case of triplets. When the young are about six months old, they ride on their mothers' backs. At the age of three, the

the males cover much more territory. A chimpanzee community is made up of subgroups of from three to six animals each. These smaller groups may be made up of related males. They may also be made up of a mother with her grown daughter and their offspring. Males leave their mothers at the age of nine years to join a group of males. Grown females sometimes leave their original community to join another one. If these

Above: Athough baby chimpanzees cling tightly to their mother's belly to travel, larger youngsters can ride piggyback!

females take a baby with them, it will not be accepted into the new group. The males of the new group will kill the young chimpanzee.

Chimpanzees spend more time grooming each other's coats than any other kind of ape. This seems to be done for the purpose of strengthening bonds among the chimpanzees. Although most grooming sessions involve two chimpanzees, groups of eight or ten apes sometimes cluster together to groom each other in a process that can take as much time as an hour or two.

There are strict ranks within the male groups. A strong chimpanzee will not hesitate to show his strength to others in his social group, or community. He will drum on tree roots with his hands and feet, and shake the branches with his hair standing up, all the while shrieking loudly. Often, two or three brothers join together in a show of strength.

The males of different ages and ranks that belong to one group will patrol the borders of their territory together. If they come upon a lookout from a neighboring community, they do not hesitate to attack the intruder, biting and throwing sticks and stones, which sometimes weigh up to 9 pounds (4 kg). In this way, chimpanzees' use of weapons is yet another way in which they are like humans.

Those that are wounded in these fights usually die or become easy prey for leopards. Sometimes the encounters can result in an all-out war between the two communities. Here again, the chimpanzees behave more like humans than like other apes.

Above: Chimpanzees will often use chewed-up leaves as a sort of sponge for drinking water; they dip the sponge in the water and then squeeze the liquid out.
Left: A young chimpanzee is cleaning a stick which it will later use to stir up a nest of termites.

Bonobos

Scientific name: Pan paniscus
Weight: 55-99 pounds (25-45 kg)
Height seated: 27.5-35.5 inches (70-90 cm)

At first glance, it is easy to mistake a bonobo for a chimpanzee. A closer look, however, shows there are several differences. For one thing, bonobos are more slender than chimpanzees. Also, their arms and legs are longer. Bonobos always have dark faces, and young chimpanzees have pale faces. In addition, bonobos have reddish lips, white hair on their posteriors, and clearer voices than chimpanzees. Bonobos are sometimes called pygmy chimpanzees. That name is misleading, however, because they are not much smaller than chimpanzees.

The bonobo lives in Zaire, a country in central Africa. A village on the banks of the Zaire River was once called Bolobo. Over time, however, the name became Bonobo, the ape's name. The Zaire River works as a border between chimpanzee and bonobo communities. The bonobos live south of the river, and the chimpanzees live north and east of it.

Thus, these two apes that look so much like each other never see one another in the wild. The bonobo was discovered in 1925 by a scientist who was intrigued by the small sizes of ape skeletons displayed in a museum in Belgium. There has been, however, less study on the bonobo than on any other ape. In the late nineteenth and early twentieth centuries, four bonobos were living in zoos. They had been mistaken for small chimpanzees. But in the late 1920s, studies of their bones showed that the bonobos were a different species.

Bonobos move through the lowland forests in groups of up to sixty animals. Within the group, there are subgroups of from one to fifteen animals. Each group covers about a mile and a half (2.5 km) a day. They almost always move about in the afternoon. Now and then they stop to eat, play, rest, and groom one another's hair. Toward evening, each animal builds a sleeping nest in a tree.

The bonobos' territory is usually about 8 square miles (20 sq km) in size. The animals constantly call out to each other, and they can detect a larger, stronger group when it is far away. The group then has plenty of time to move away.

Before noon, the animals stay in trees, usually climbing about 39 to 59 feet (12-18 m) high. Sometimes they climb as high as 100 feet (30 m). They feel safer in the trees than on the ground. When threatened, they flee into the trees rather than trying to get away on the ground. Their main enemy is the leopard. From time to time, a young bonobo will be attacked by an eagle or a rock python. The animals are occasionally hunted by humans for their meat.

Opposite and right: Unlike chimpanzees, bonobos always have dark faces and sideburns. They are sometimes referred to as pygmy chimpanzees, but this is misleading since bonobos are only slightly smaller than their cousins.

Bonobos spend about one-third of their day eating. They especially like fruit, but they also eat leaves, seeds, shoots, plant pith, and mushrooms. They may also eat worms, insects, and honey. Males sometimes hunt and eat young antelopes. No one in the group ever goes hungry because the animals always share their food. The native people of Zaire aren't happy when they see a hungry group of bonobos, because the animals can quickly ruin sugar cane and banana crops.

Every three or four years, the female gives birth to one baby. The gestation period is eight months. Males always stay with the same group, but females often change groups.

Why Study Apes?

American scientist Clarence Ray Carpenter was one of the first researchers who wanted to know more about the way apes live in the wild. He began his studies of white-handed gibbons in the forests of Southeast Asia in 1937. Many other researchers followed his example. Best known among these are three women who all happened to study under the famous British paleontologist and natural scientist, Louis Leakey.

English ethologist Jane Goodall began studying chimpanzees in Gombe National Park in Tanzania in 1960. After several years, the animals accepted her as a friend, as the photograph above shows. In 1967,

American zoologist Dian Fossey began a similar project with mountain gorillas in Rwanda, a country in east-central Africa. She lived for many years among the "gentle giants." The third researcher is Canadian Biruté Galdikas. She has been studying orangutans on Borneo since 1971. These three women produced the first long-term studies of apes living in the wild.

What good is all this research on apes? Among other things, it helps us understand animals that are threatened with extinction. We will best be able to protect these animals only after we more fully understand their needs and habits.

APPENDIX
TO
ANIMAL FAMILIES

APES

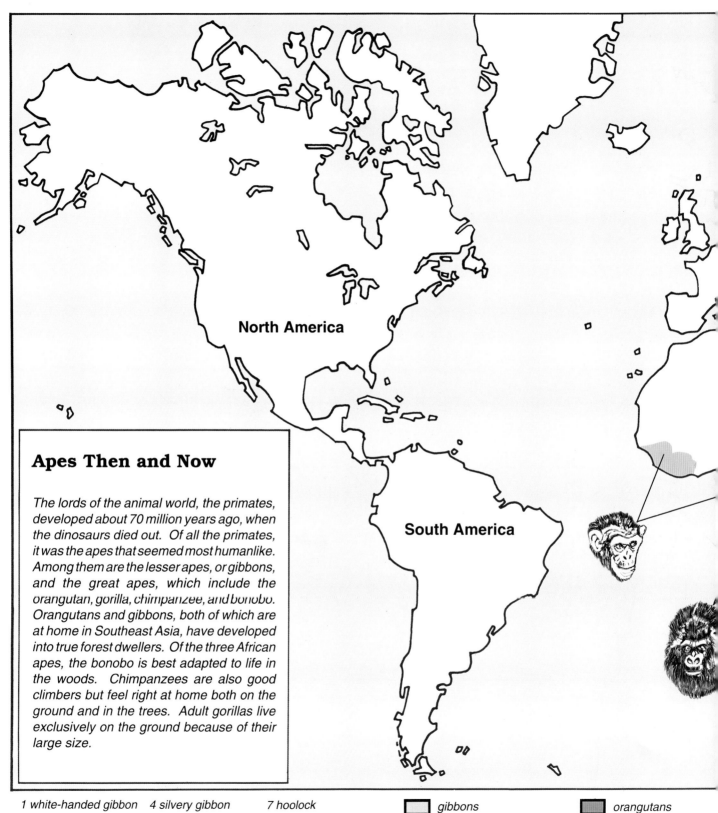

North America

South America

Apes Then and Now

The lords of the animal world, the primates, developed about 70 million years ago, when the dinosaurs died out. Of all the primates, it was the apes that seemed most humanlike. Among them are the lesser apes, or gibbons, and the great apes, which include the orangutan, gorilla, chimpanzee, and bonobo. Orangutans and gibbons, both of which are at home in Southeast Asia, have developed into true forest dwellers. Of the three African apes, the bonobo is best adapted to life in the woods. Chimpanzees are also good climbers but feel right at home both on the ground and in the trees. Adult gorillas live exclusively on the ground because of their large size.

1 white-handed gibbon   4 silvery gibbon   7 hoolock   ▢ gibbons   ▢ orangutans
2 agile gibbon   5 capped gibbon   8 white-cheeked gibbon
3 gray gibbon   6 Kloss' gibbon   9 siamang

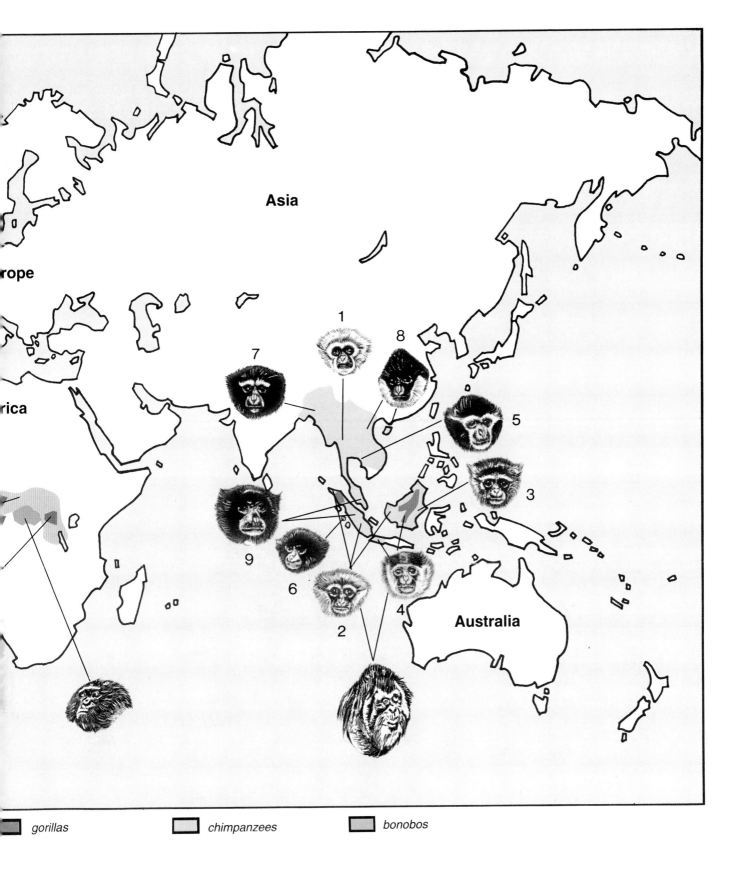

Asia

Europe

Africa

Australia

1
7
8
5
3
9
6
4
2

gorillas   chimpanzees   bonobos

ABOUT THESE BOOKS

Although this series is called "Animal Families," these books aren't just about fathers, mothers, and young. They also discuss the scientific definition of *family,* which is a division of biological classification and includes many animals.

Biological classification is a method that scientists use to identify and organize living things. Using this system, scientists place animals and plants into larger groups that share similar characteristics. Characteristics are physical features, natural habits, ancestral backgrounds, or any other qualities that make one organism either like or different from another.

The method used today for biological classification was introduced in 1753 by a Swedish botanist-naturalist named Carolus Linnaeus. Although many scientists tried to find ways to classify the world's plants and animals, Linnaeus's system seemed to be the only useful choice. Charles Darwin, a famous British naturalist, referred to Linnaeus's system in his theory of evolution, which was published in his book *On the Origin of Species* in 1859. Linnaeus's system of classification, shown below, includes seven major categories, or groups. These are: kingdom, phylum, class, order, family, genus, and species.

An easy way to remember the divisions and their order is to memorize this sentence: "Ken Put Cake On Frank's Good Shirt." The first letter of each word in this sentence gives you the first letter of a division. (The *K* in *Ken,* for example, stands for *kingdom.*) The order of the words in this sentence suggests the order of the divisions from largest to smallest. The kingdom is the largest of these divisions; the species is the smallest. The larger the division, the more types of animals or plants it contains. For example, the animal kingdom, called Animalia, contains everything from worms to whales. Smaller divisions, such as the family, have fewer members that share more characteristics. For example, members of the bear family, Ursidae, include the polar bear, the brown bear, and many others.

In the following chart, the lion species is followed through all seven categories. As the categories expand to include more and more members, remember that only a few examples are pictured here. Each division has many more members.

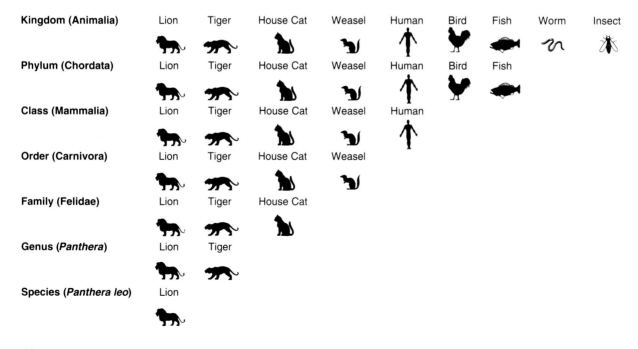

Kingdom (Animalia)	Lion	Tiger	House Cat	Weasel	Human	Bird	Fish	Worm	Insect
Phylum (Chordata)	Lion	Tiger	House Cat	Weasel	Human	Bird	Fish		
Class (Mammalia)	Lion	Tiger	House Cat	Weasel	Human				
Order (Carnivora)	Lion	Tiger	House Cat	Weasel					
Family (Felidae)	Lion	Tiger	House Cat						
Genus (*Panthera*)	Lion	Tiger							
Species (*Panthera leo*)	Lion								

SCIENTIFIC NAMES OF THE ANIMALS IN THIS BOOK

Animals have different names in every language. For this reason, researchers the world over use the same scientific names, which usually stem from ancient Greek or Latin. Most animals are classified by two names. One is the genus name; the other is the name of the species to which they belong. Additional names indicate further subgroupings. Here is a list of the animals included in *Apes:*

White-handed gibbon .... *Hylobates lar*
Agile gibbon .... *Hylobates agilis*
Gray gibbon .... *Hylobates muelleri*
Silvery gibbon .... *Hylobates moloch*
Capped gibbon .... *Hylobates pileatus*
Kloss' gibbon .... *Hylobates klossi*
Hoolock .... *Hylobates hoolock*

White-cheeked gibbon .... *Hylobates concolor*
Siamang .... *Symphalangus syndactylus*
Orangutan .... *Pongo pygmaeus*
Gorilla .... *Gorilla gorilla*
Chimpanzee .... *Pan troglodytes*
Bonobo .... *Pan paniscus*

GLOSSARY

ancestors
Persons from whom one is descended; a predecessor.

anthropoid
Resembling humans; humanlike.

bonobo
Originally called "pygmy chimpanzee," the bonobo is an ape generally smaller in size than the chimpanzee and lives in the swampy forests of Zaire. The bonobo is now an endangered species.

brachiate
To swing by the arms from branch to branch.

chimpanzee
A large ape of tropical Africa having a brown-to-black coat, relatively hairless face with rounded muzzle, prominent ears, and hands adapted for knuckle-walking. The chimpanzee is noted for its intelligence and humanlike behavior.

class
The third of seven divisions in the biological classification system proposed by Swedish botanist-naturalist Carolus Linnaeus. The class is the main subdivision of the phylum. Apes belong to the class Mammalia. Animals in this class, which includes humans, share certain features: they have skin covered with hair, they give birth to live young, and they nourish the young with milk from mammary glands.

deforestation
To cut down or clear away trees and forests.

endangered species
A group of animals that have become rare and are threatened with extinction, usually because of human behavior or a change in environmental conditions.

ethologist
A scientist who studies the behavior of animals in their natural surroundings or habitats.

evolutionary development
A gradual process in which something changes into a different and usually more complex or better form; a theory that groups such as species may change with time so that descendants differ from their ancestors.

extinction
The condition of being completely destroyed or killed off. Many animals, like the dodo, are now extinct.

family
The fifth of seven divisions in the biological classification system proposed by Swedish botanist-naturalist Carolus Linnaeus. A family is the main subdivision of the order and contains one or more genera. Apes belong to the family Pongidae.

foliage
The leaves of a plant.

fossils
Any remains, impressions, or traces of a living thing of a former geological age.

genus (plural: **genera**)
The sixth division in the biological classification system proposed by Swedish botanist-naturalist Carolus Linnaeus. A genus is the main subdivision of a family and includes one or more species.

gestation period
The number of days from actual conception to the birth of an animal. Gestation periods vary greatly for different types of animals.

gibbon
A small, slender, long-armed ape of southeastern Asia and the East Indies that lives in trees.

gorilla
A very large, long-armed ape found in Africa; the largest of the primates.

habitat
The natural living area or environment in which an animal usually lives.

kingdom
The first of seven divisions in the biological classification system proposed by Swedish botanist-naturalist Carolus Linnaeus. Animals, including humans, belong to the kingdom Animalia. It is one of five kingdoms.

liana
A woody vine that may climb as high as the trees in a tropical forest.

mammal
A warm-blooded animal that nurses its young with its own milk. Whales, humans, and apes are some examples of mammals.

mate (verb)
To join together (animals) to produce offspring.

orangutan
A large ape of the forests of Borneo and Sumatra that has very long arms and long, shaggy, reddish brown hair. Orangutans live mostly in trees and eat mainly fruits and leaves.

order
The fourth of seven divisions in the biological classification system proposed by the Swedish botanist-naturalist Carolus Linnaeus. The order is the main subdivision of the class and contains many different families. Apes belong to the order of Primates.

paleontologist
A scientist who studies the past by looking closely at fossils and other remains.

phylum (plural: **phyla**)
The second of seven divisions in the biological classification system proposed by the Swedish botanist-naturalist Carolus Linnaeus. A phylum is one of the main divisions of a kingdom. Apes belong to the phylum Chordata, the group consisting mainly of animals with backbones (vertebrates).

pith
The central spongy tissue of plant stems.

primates
Any of the highest order of animals including monkeys, apes, and humans that are distinguished by the ability to use their hands and to interact socially.

savanna
A flat, treeless grassland of tropical or subtropical regions; a treeless plain.

species
The last of seven divisions in the biological classification system proposed by Swedish botanist-naturalist Carolus Linnaeus. The species is the main subdivision of the genus. It may include further subgroups of its own, called subspecies. At the level of species, members share many features and are capable of breeding with one another.

zoologist
A scientist who studies the biology of animals and the way they live.

MORE BOOKS ABOUT APES

Apes. Helen Kay (Macmillan)
The Chimpanzee Family Book. Jane Goodall (Picture Book Studio)
The Gorilla. Carl R. Green and William R. Sanford (Crestwood House)
Gorilla. Robert M. McClung (William Morrow)
My Life with Chimpanzees. Jane Goodall (Atheneum)
Orangutan: Endangered Ape. Aline Amon (Atheneum)
Seymour, A Gibbon. Phyllis Borea (Atheneum)
Watching the Wild Apes. Bettyann Kevles (E. P. Dutton)

PLACES TO WRITE

The following are some of the many organizations that exist to educate people about animals, promote the protection of animals, and encourage the conservation of their environments. Write to these organizations for more information about apes, other animals, or animal concerns of interest to you. When you write, include your name, address, and age, and tell them clearly what you want to know. Don't forget to enclose a stamped, self-addressed envelope for a reply.

African Wildlife Foundation
Mountain Gorilla Project
1717 Massachusetts Ave. NW
Washington, DC 20036

Animal Protection Institute
P.O. Box 22505
Sacramento, California 95822

Jane Goodall Institute for Wildlife
 Research, Education, and
 Conservation
P.O. Box 26846
Tucson, Arizona 85726

Wildlife Preservation Trust International
34th Street and Girard Avenue
Philadelphia, Pennsylvania 19104

World Wildlife Fund (Canada)
90 Eglinton Avenue East, Suite 504
Toronto, Ontario M4P 2Z7

THINGS TO DO

These projects are designed to help you have fun with what you've learned about apes. You can do them alone, in small groups, or as a class project.

1. Spend a day at the zoo. Find the apes exhibit. Can you identify any of them? Also, listen to the "songs" of the apes. How many different tunes can you hear?

2. Observe the facial features of apes in books, on television, at an art gallery or museum, or at the zoo. What emotions do you see? Do the apes seem happy, sad, frightened, angry, or curious? How else might you describe their expressions?

3. Make two columns on a sheet of paper. In one column, list the characteristics of apes that are *similar* to humans. In the other column, list the ways apes *differ* from humans. Which list is longer?

4. Construct a chart of ape facts. List the names of all the apes in a column moving from smallest to largest. Across the top of the chart, add columns for items such as weight, height, color of hair, gestation period, habitat, and any other category you think might be useful to a study of apes.

INDEX